Bobby Normal
And The
Children of Cain

A.S.Chambers

First Published Basilisk Books 2022
This edition published in 2024.
Copyright © 2024 Basilisk Books.

Cover art © 2022 Liam Shaw.

ISBN: 978-1-915679-51-2

Dedication

This book is dedicated to children everywhere who have had their lives ruined by the horrors of war.

A huge thank you to everyone who kindly backed my Kickstarter campaign for this book. Special mentions go to Ron Chick, Simon Brindley, Debs McGowan, Robyn, Lee, Rohanna, Rebecca Armstrong,

Also, special thanks to the Seraph tier members of my Book Club for their valued support:
Paul Lewis
Gemma Innes.

For more details about my Book Club and how you can receive signed copies of my books when they are published, please visit my website:
www.aschambers.co.uk.

Also a huge thank you, once again, to Liam Shaw for his amazing cover art.

Ebook short stories.
High Moon - 2013
Girls Just Wanna Have Fun – 2013
Needs Must - 2019

Novellas.
Songbird – 2019
Bobby Normal and The Eternal Talisman - 2021
Bobby Normal and the Virtuous Man - 2021
Bobby Normal and the Fallen - 2023
Bobby Normal and the Black Dragon – 2024
Child of Light - Due 2024
Child of Fire - Due 2025

Omnibuses.
Children of Cain - 2019
Macabre Collection: Volume One - 2022
Macabre Collection: Volume Two - 2023
Sam Spallucci Omnibus: Volume One - 2022
Sam Spallucci Omnibus: Volume Two - 2023

CONTENTS

Previously...

Bobby, a teenage boy from the village of Irlingbury, and Katy, his outspoken eight-year-old sister, were entrusted with the Eternal Talisman by a girl named Persephone. On their travels to the neighbouring village of Orchester, they were hounded by Teller, a bully from their home village whose father was a servant of Kanor, the being that had brought about the Divergence which had decimated humanity, reducing it to a pitiful remnant that lived in constant fear of death. Things came to a head when Katy pushed Teller from a bridge, leading to his gruesome death — a death for which the young girl showed no apparent remorse.

Upon arriving in Orchester, the siblings

successfully delivered the Eternal Talisman to Jason, the individual that Persephone had believed to be the Man of Virtue, the only person that could overthrow Kanor. Jason persuaded them to join his followers on a mission to destroy a group of constructs, the clay-based lifeforms that were the murderous servants of Kanor. The assault ended in tragedy with Katy and Bobby being the only ones to escape with their lives after the old man known as Cutter saved them from a cunning Shadow Wraith.

After Bobby had a dream about a shadowy warrior named Claw fighting an army of constructs, the children returned to Orchester where they found themselves accused of treachery. Jason claimed that they were in fact constructs and instructed that they should be burned at the stake. They were snatched from the jaws of death by three mysterious strangers, one of whom was Claw, the brave warrior from Bobby's dream.

We rejoin them as they travel away from Orchester and back towards their home village of Irlingbury…

Chapter One

Right about now, Bobby was feeling decidedly unsure of things.

It could have been any number of the weird and decidedly dangerous life-altering events of the past week that were causing him his current consternation, but it wasn't.

It was something far more immediate, far more terrifying.

With every pounding hoofbeat from the large brown horse beneath him, Bobby was convinced that he would soon be departing this mortal world in a terribly agonising manner, thrown from a great height and trampled over by the demonic beast upon which he was currently travelling.

"You're sure this is safe?" he asked the blonde woman around whose waist he had his arms tightly locked in a life-preserving grip.

She glanced over her shoulder, her long hair flicking to one side, and just smiled.

That was not reassuring to the green-faced teenager.

Bobby held on even tighter as the horse beneath him steadily pounded its feet along the rutted and worn track along which he and his kid sister Katy had walked in the opposite direction just a week previous. Bobby, being the impoverished orphan of a widowed woodworker, had never before ridden on a horse. To Bobby, the large equine beasts symbolised just one thing: privilege. And with privilege came subservience to Kanor and his hierarchy of fear. The only humans he had ever seen riding horses had been Teller and his father or their cronies and associates. Aside from that, the only other individuals he had ever seen travelling in this fashion had been the merciless Shadow Wraiths. As a result, horses, for Bobby, were things to be feared, not trusted.

This lack of trust was reinforced with

every precarious jolt that the beast took, threatening to tumble him to a bone-shattering impact on the road below, as they continued on their nighttime journey.

"Hey, kid!"

Gripping the blonde woman's waist and keeping the side of his face resolutely fixed against the long cloak that she wore, Bobby ventured to turn his head to the right. He peered over to the image in front of him that bounced up and down in an overwhelmingly nauseating manner. It was the other of the two women, the one with short red hair. She was grinning at him as Katy sat behind her bouncing up and down on the horse with utter glee.

"What?" Bobby squeaked.

"I told you earlier, Scorpion don't say much. No point asking her questions."

"Oh. Okay."

"But," the redhead continued, her green eyes twinkling in the moonlight, "in answer to your inquiry: mostly."

Mostly? What was *that* supposed to mean? Bobby gripped Scorpion even tighter and felt her body judder as she laughed silently to herself.

"Come on, Bobby," the redhead continued, obviously taking great glee in the boy's discomfort. "Lighten up. Your kid sister's certainly enjoying herself. Ain't that right, Katy?"

Katy nodded emphatically, "Yes!" she squealed. "Can we go faster?"

The redhead laughed. "Course we can!" She snapped her reins and yelled something unintelligible at her mount, caus-ing the horse to whinny in excitement and bolt forwards. The eight-year-old girl on its back shrieked with utter glee as her long, knotted hair flew out behind her.

Bobby just squeezed his eyes tight shut and buried his face into Scorpion's fair hair as he prayed for the torture to end.

"Don't you mind Tigress. She's just try-ing to lighten you up."

Carefully, Bobby cracked open one tentative eye and looked over at the third and final horse rider of the party, the man who called himself Claw. "She's not suc-ceeding," Bobby grumbled.

The sandy-haired man considered

Bobby's words before replying. "I think they did things differently when she was your age."

The teenage boy frowned. "I can't believe things have changed *that* much since she was a child. She's only in her twenties."

Claw gave an amused snort.

"What?"

Again, the man seemed to carefully consider his words before answering. "Looks can be deceptive."

Bobby definitely couldn't argue with that. In the last few days, he had encountered an old man who could turn into a wolf, a Shadow Wraith that could transform its arms into deadly weapons and now these three curious strangers who could run faster than he could perceive. "Tell me about it."

"How old do you think I am?"

Bobby eyed his companion up and down. "Somewhere between thirty and forty years or so?"

Claw's eyes twinkled amusement in the moonlight. "Bobby, I was born over two thousand years ago. Scorpion, with whom you are riding is over four thousand years old and Tigress… Well, we're not entirely sure because she was born before calendars were really a thing, but a good guess would be about five thousand plus."

All of a sudden, Bobby's primal fear of horseback riding dissipated into the night sky like steam from a pot that has come to the boil over a campfire. He sat up straight and looked Claw in the face, trying to discern whether or not the man was teasing him in an attempt to take his mind off the torturous journey. His father, Howard, had always said that it was a wise thing to look into people's eyes when they told you something that you did not expect to hear; it would give you an insight into the validity of their words and the truth of their intentions. As he stared into the brown eyes of the man who claimed to be older than Bobby could even comprehend, he saw no hint of mirth or deception.

"How?" he finally asked.

Claw opened his mouth to reply, but his attention was diverted to the sound of Tigress and Katy galloping back along the road towards them. Bobby followed his gaze and could not fail to see that a darkness had erased all traces of mirth from the woman's face.

"What is it?" Claw asked her.

"Trouble."

Until Bobby and Katy had been rescued from an irate Teller by Persephone, the girl who had entrusted them with the Eternal Talisman, neither of them had set foot outside of their home village of Irlingbury. Sure, they had known that there was a world outside of their microcosm, but it had not really interested them that much.

Irlingbury had been their home.

Katy, Bobby felt, had always had a simpler relationship with the place than he did. She had never known their mother plus their father had died when she was very young, so the majority of her life which she could remember had been spent with just Bobby. To his sister, Irlingbury was a place she existed with her brother. They lived by their wits, scavenging or stealing food when they could and running whenever was necessary.

For Bobby, his views on the place of his birth were more complex and fell into three distinct phases.

He remembered a period when things had been much simpler, when he had been truly happy and content in Irlingbury. This was the time when his mother had still been alive. His earliest memories were of helping her tend the neat vegetable patch that she had cultivated behind their small, homely cottage. He would toddle around the garden, picking weeds out from between the vegetables as his mother instructed him, then they would pull the fully grown produce that they would eat that evening. She would hold his hand in hers, soft skin with finger-tips that had been roughened from constant gardening and housework, and she would lead him to the hearth where she would sing softly as she chopped the vegetables and cooked them in a pot over the fire, ready for when his father came back from market.

This stopped suddenly when Katy had been born.

His mother had died in childbirth. Bobby had listened as the midwife had explained to his father that the baby had been problematic, facing the wrong way. There had been a lot of blood lost, and the last thing that his mother had seen had been the child which she had just brought into the world.

She had held Katy in her arms, closed her eyes and fallen asleep as if tired from the exertion, never to waken.

This brought the second phase in Bobby's relationship with Irlingbury, one of hard work but a feeling of accomplishment. The first few months after his mother's death had been terribly hard. His father had needed to adjust to a new routine of life. He had become a familiar figure around town, carrying not only his handmade goods but also a newborn baby that had been constantly nestled in a sling on his chest. And, always by his side, was the young, serious-faced lad who was his constant companion and aide. However, even with Bobby there to carry what Howard could not fit on his back and to assist with small jobs and customers when Katy demanded his father's attention, it was obvious to all in the village that the widower was not coping with the sudden, dramatic change in his domestic arrangements. The young Bobby noticed that in the year following his mother's death, his father seemed to age considerably more than twelve months, his face becoming drawn and his skin slack.

Neighbours suggested to Howard that he take another wife, a young girl who would do as she was told and would look after the *young 'uns* while he went about his work. But the woodworker resolutely refused. He said that he had only intended to wed the once and he would not dishonour Ruth's grave by wedding again. So he would work his finger to the bone in his workshop whilst caring for and feeding his two children.

Things came to a head when Howard was taken ill. Bobby woke one morning to the sound of an infant Katy shouting for her father. He ventured downstairs and found his dad asleep in a chair in front of a dead fire, his skin chilled and clammy. Howard had fallen asleep there the previous night, too weak to make it to bed. Bobby guided him upstairs and helped him to settle under his sheets, watching fretfully as the man drifted off to a feverish sleep. The boy then took his sister by the hand and led her out into the vegetable patch that he had used to tend with their mother. It was wilder now; his father was not much of a gardener. Weeds grew around the garden, but there were still some persistent root vegetables there that could be dug up, cooked and eaten. So, Bobby set to, settling Katy down in a small patch of earth, letting her play with the worms and bugs, trying not to think about how many went in her mouth. A few hours later, he had prepared a hearty stew which he and Katy took up to their father.

"Did you make this?" Howard asked as he devoured the meal.

Bobby nodded. "Is it good?"

His father presented him the empty bowl, a weary smile on his fatigued face. "I think we need to have a rethink about how we do things around here."

And so it was that, for the next few years, whilst Howard turned wood and created goods to sell, Bobby was the one that tended the garden, kept the house clean and watched over his infant sister as she continued to grow in both height and appetite. It became a time of contentment as the three of them settled into this new type of life. He found it immensely rewarding, making their little house a welcoming home once more.

Then the Shadow Wraiths rode into the village and his life in Irlingbury entered the third phase.

Howard was labelled a traitor and summarily executed. Teller's father had not hesitated to inflict even more cruel punishment on the newly orphaned children. When Bobby and Katy managed to get back to their cottage, they found their home aflame. All of their father's materials had been stacked up against the small house and had been set alight. The garden, which the two of them had meticulously tended, had been trampled over, the vegetables ripped out of the ground and pulverised under foot and hoof.

Bobby had just stood and watched the flames rise, smoke curling its way up into the air.

Just as he did this evening on the road that led into Irlingbury.

Bobby, Katy and their three companions stood at the edge of town and watched the flames rise into the night sky as the entire village burned.

A.S.Chambers

Chapter Two

Bobby did not sleep well that night. Claw had said that nothing could be achieved from him and Katy stumbling around a ruined village as sleep tried to drag them to their bed. "You would just hurt yourselves," he had explained. "There is nothing you can do for your village, so you must tend to yourselves." He had located a copse of trees on the outskirts of town and had sat down with them as they had settled down to sleep. The last thing Bobby saw as his eyes drifted shut was Scorpion and Tigress heading off towards the smoke and flame.

It was the smoke and flame that dominated his dreams that night. He found himself staggering around the back alleys of

Irlingbury, coughing and spluttering as the acrid fumes from burning cottages filled his tortured lungs. In the distance, through the gloom, he could make out Katy running just ahead of him, almost out of sight. He made after his kid sister, but every time he found himself closing in on her, she darted around a corner, giggling and laughing, oblivious to the burning ruins that surrounded her. Bobby lurched forwards, his arms outstretched, in part as an attempt to grab his younger sibling, in part to stop himself from stumbling in the chaos of the devastated village. All around him, people were screaming as they ran from the flames, bundles of belongings grasped desperately in their arms.

Then, above in the night sky, Bobby heard something which chilled him to the core, even in the searing heat of the inferno.

A primordial screeching filled the midnight sky as the sound of long black wings clapped in the air. Bobby stopped running, turned to look up and saw the obsidian silhouette of a gigantic dragon soar in front of the pale, white moon. It circled above, turned its head towards the village and let loose a fireball from its screaming mouth. The villagers fell helplessly to their knees in terror and were immolated by the roaring breath from the monstrous creature. Bobby watched, sickened, as their skin blistered and peeled from their bones, before their skeletons were reduced to ash in the over-whelming heat.

Bobby made to run but found that he could not move. Thick arms of clay were bound around him, holding him fast to a stout pole set amid a pile of kindling and fire-wood. The arms of the constructs tightened as he tried to wriggle free and he could not escape as the fire crept up the base of the pyre and began to lick hungrily at his cloth-ing.

As the flames started to catch at his skin, he saw Katy again across the other side of the village square. She was not alone. His sister was holding the hand of a tall, elegant, dark-haired woman. Bobby cried out from amongst the flames, begging the woman to save him, but the stranger smiled wickedly, turned and, taking Katy with her, walked away in the light of the full moon.

Bobby twisted and writhed against the immovable arms of the construct that held him fast.

He watched in horror as the creature's arms baked solid.

Then the flames cracked, leapt up and engulfed him.

Bobby awoke with a start.

The sound of the cracking carried across the small clearing once more and he frantically patted at his clothes, his face, terrified that he was burning. Instead of fire and scorched burns, he just found cold, chilled skin. He shivered as he pulled his fraught mind together and seated himself up under his blanket.

"I'm sorry. Did I wake you?"

Bobby frowned as his sleep encumbered brain tried to drag itself up to speed with its surroundings. It was later in the day than he had expected, the sun having passed its zenith. Katy snored resolutely next to him. Across the other side of the copse, Claw was stood, heavily cloaked, a long whip in his gloved hand. A reasonable distance away from him, set upon a fallen tree were propped small pieces of wood.

"I was practising," the man explained. As if to demonstrate, he let fly across the clearing the silver tip of the whip and one of the targets shot off into the surrounding trees.

Bobby eased himself up from the floor. "Impressive," he noted.

Claw quietly nodded his thanks. In the depths of his cowl, his brow furrowed. "You were dreaming. Nightmares?"

The teenager forced the images of his disturbed sleep out of his mind and gave an approximation of a nonchalant shrug. "My waking time seems to be one long nightmare at the moment. Why should my sleep be any different?"

The cloaked man stood silently regarding him. His brown eyes peering intently out of the gloom of his hood. He nodded. "I know what you mean. There was someone I knew many years ago. His life…" He shook his head. "It was turned upside down. The day-to-day became a collection of the bizarre, the crazy. He suffered so much at night with dreams. He saw things that no one should see."

"What happened to him?"

The man slid his tongue over his lips as his brown eyes held Bobby.

"Would you like to have a go?"

Bobby frowned. "Pardon?"

Claw curled the whip up into his gloved hand. "It's quite simple," he explained, gesturing for Bobby to come and stand by his side. "It's all about acquiring the most speed at the tip."

Bobby frowned. "I don't know. The last time I got up close with one of those wasn't very pleasant."

The man nodded. "I find it is important to not let your past dominate your future." Once more he gestured to a spot by his side.

Bobby looked again at the weapon. His hand rose to a small scratch just below his eye before he stretched, ran his fingers through his unkempt hair and walked over to the cloaked Claw.

"Come and stand here," the man gestured to a spot on his left, "and watch what I do."

Bobby stood where he was told and observed carefully as the long whip was unravelled from its coil. Claw's hands expertly flicked it outwards in small movements until the long stretch of leather lay in a straight line behind him. He reached his arm out past his shoulder and flexed his gloved grip on the solid handle of the weapon.

"It's all about timing and momentum," he explained. He snapped his hand forward and Bobby let out a cry of excitement as the silver talon at the end of the leather cord smashed a piece of wood off the fallen tree. Claw began to wind the whip back. "Okay?"

Bobby just grinned in excitement.

Claw smiled and handed him the weapon, moving carefully to the boy's left-hand side. "So," he explained, "gently flick it out to extend the material. Feel the weight as you do so; balance it in your hand. Familiarise yourself with a weapon. You should never use a weapon that you don't understand. It will harm you more than those at whom you are aiming."

Bobby nodded as he studied the long weapon. He carefully ran his fingertips over the corded leather, feeling the tightness of its structure until he reached the silver barb at the end — a simple metal hook tied into the end of the whip. He winced as he prodded its curved tip. "It's really sharp. Did you make this yourself?"

Claw gave a *so-so* gesture with his hand. "I made the whip, but the barb I acquired on the day the constructs rose. It's what gave me my name."

Bobby's attention switched from the weapon to the man who was hidden under the deep hood. "You were there? When Kanor destroyed humanity?"

Claw nodded.

The boy swallowed. "What… what was it like?"

Even in the dark shadows of the hood the emotions on the man's face were clear to see. He was no longer looking at a teenage boy in a clearing in a wood. His brow was knotted, his lips compressed and his sight was focussed elsewhere.

"It was brutal," he eventually managed. "I was a different person before Kanor came. We all were." His shoulders rose and fell and his lips moved as if he were emitting a melancholy sigh, but Bobby noted that, even stood close to him, there was no sound of expulsion of air, nor the feel of the man's breath on his skin. "That was a long time ago," Claw continued, the corner of his eyes relaxing. "Let's concentrate on this whip, shall we?"

Bobby nodded silently and began to gently move his hand in a rhythmic flicking motion. He watched in fascination as the cord of leather seemed to take on a life of its own, the silver talon snaking like a stealthy predator through the grass. "It's really heavy," he said, noting the weight of the handle in his grip.

"That keeps it grounded," Claw explained. "And you, too. It makes you aware that you are holding something that can actually kill individuals, should you desire it." His brown, hooded eyes watched as the whip reached its full length. "Good. Now just give it a couple of gentle shakes. Feel how it moves."

Bobby did as he was instructed and watched the whip ripple through the patchy grass. Its long structure undulated, causing the silver tip to flick left and right. "It looks alive."

"Back when I was younger, before the Divergence, I knew this cat. He was black and malicious. His tail would flick like that before he pounced on you and drew blood."

Bobby's attention was drawn from the whip to the face of his tutor. "A *cat*? What's that?"

The shoulders of the hooded man rose and fell. "Sorry. I forget how much of the old world has disappeared, died out. It was a small creature that lived with humans. They were originally predators that humans domesticated to hunt down rats and the like, but being smart, they wheedled their way in front of the fireplace. This cat was one of the shrewdest creatures that I ever knew."

"I could have done with him a few days ago," Bobby said. "I had a rather horrid encounter with some rats in a sewer."

"Not pleasant," said Claw.

"Not pleasant," Bobby concurred.

"So, back to the whip. Stretch your arm backwards and be aware of the connection from the shoulder to your wrist. The strong shoulder muscles will give the whip power as you thrust it forwards, the wrist will give it precision and guidance. Go for it."

Bobby flexed his hand on the grip and rotated his shoulder to unkink the muscles that had knotted up from his restless sleep on the hard floor. He felt his heart begin to beat faster with excitement and his breathing increased in rapidity. He jerked the whip forward and watched its shining barb smack into the ground in front of the tree trunk. He grimaced.

"Hey, don't be hard on yourself," Claw smiled as Bobby disconsolately wound the weapon back into his hand. "It was your first go and a good effort. You just need to bear in mind two things. First, is the trajectory of the tip. It needs to flick around and be fully extended. That gives it the fullest momentum and speed. Rather like putting a starship into a slingshot manoeuvre around the sun." He paused as Bobby frowned in confusion. "Don't worry," Claw apologised, shaking his head. "It's an old reference. Just make sure that the tip comes all the way around. When you threw it that time, it sort of snaked past your head. You were lucky you didn't take your ear off," he winked. "The other thing you need to be aware of is what your body is doing when you crack the whip. Time it so that you sling the whip between breaths. That keeps it steady. I forgot to mention that. It's not something I have to think about." Again, Bobby frowned and Claw motioned to the whip: "Go on. Try again."

Bobby let out a deep breath and concentrated on his breathing as he slid the whip out in small, gentle gestures. He felt the cool afternoon air seep down into his lungs and the warm recycled air expel through his mouth. Three times he repeated this until the whip was at full length then, pausing the breathing cycle, he flicked the whip round in a full, horizontal arc. A sharp crack filled the glen and a piece of wood flew off into the thicket behind.

The teenage boy whooped with exultation as he punched the air with the handle of the whip. "Yes!" he cried. "I did it!"

"Looks like you've been working up an appetite," came an amused voice from over his shoulder.

Bobby turned to see Tigress and Scorpion, both cloaked like Claw, enter the clearing, carrying packages in their arms. "Good job we found some food for you."

A tired yawn emanated from the small bundle that was a waking eight-year-old girl. "Did someone mention food?" Katy asked.

Bobby and Katy tucked into the simple meal with ravenous gratitude. They hadn't eaten since the stew that the old man Cutter had cooked for them after he had rescued them from the Shadow Wraith. There wasn't much in the way of variety in the ingredients. They were mainly scraps of meat, some fruit and a few vegetables that the women had managed to scavenge from the ruins of the village. "There wasn't much left unburnt, I'm afraid," Tigress had apologised. However, the two siblings were used to surviving on other people's throwaways, so the randomly concocted meal that afternoon was more than sufficient.

It was, however, as Katy was going back for her third attack at the small pile of apples, that Bobby lay a hand on hers and whispered, "You should leave some for the others. They haven't touched anything yet."

The small girl frowned but nodded in acceptance and drew back from the food.

"It's okay," Claw said from where he was sitting with his back to a tree, idly running the length of his whip through his gloved fingers. "You two fill yourselves up."

"But surely you need to eat something?" Bobby asked as Katy just pounced on two more pieces of fruit.

Claw's hood moved from side to side. "We're fine. Go on. Eat."

Bobby felt his stomach rumble and did as he was instructed, rejoining his sister in the consumption of the food. As he did, he let his eyes study the three strangers. There was something about them, something unusual. He didn't know exactly what, but something about them *disturbed* him. Claw sat quietly and methodically inspecting the cords of his whip, checking the weapon over for wear and tear. Tigress, the redhead, sat propped against another tree, deep in her own cloak. The blonde, Scorpion was laying with her own hooded head on the other woman's lap. Tigress' gloved hand slowly and affectionately stroked the thick material. Her lips moved rhythmically and, as he listened, Bobby could make out musical words drifting across the clearing, but they were none that he recognised.

What was it about them that troubled him? He thought back to things that Claw had said about their ages. Could they all be as old as he had claimed? Back in Irlingbury, the oldest person he had known was Old Agatha. She had been an elderly widow who had outlived not just her husband but also her three children. With no family to speak of, she had lived in a small cottage on her own, resolutely independent and accepting no charity from anyone. She was a regular sight around town, haggling the best deal from the market traders and chasing "young ruffians" with a heavy walking stick that was as gnarled and as grooved as the wrinkles on her deeply tanned face. Katy had once said that her skin resembled the texture of an apple that had been left in the sun too long, shrivelling up into itself as all its moisture left its flesh.

These three individuals were no Old Agathas! They appeared young and strong. Not to mention they were so fast. When they had rescued them from Jason's clutches, the speed at which they had travelled had been incalculable.

But, Bobby told himself, *they have not harmed us. They rescued us and have cared for us.*

So why did something inside of his gut feel like it had eaten a rancid piece of cheese?

"What are you singing?" Katy's question cut across his worried musings as she got up and sat next to Tigress and Scorpion. "It's very pretty but I don't know the words."

The redhead paused her tune and smiled from the depths of her cowl. "It's a lullaby for my loved one."

"You mean Scorpion?"

Tigress nodded, her fingers idly plucking a stray blonde hair from her partner's hood. "The words of the song are very old indeed. That's why you didn't understand them."

"Where did you learn it then?"

"My mother taught it to me when I was very little."

Katy sighed. "I never knew my mother. She died when I was born."

Tigress' green eyes fixed upon the small girl from the shadows of her hood. "I'm sorry to hear that. Mine died when I was young. The sun had passed full circle around the stones just seven times, I was told. It changes you, not having your mother around. It makes you more independent, but something is always missing. There's a gap in your heart that needs filling, isn't there? I was on my own for many years after she went to join my ancestors. I got into trouble." A mischievous grin spread across her red lips. "A *lot* of trouble. The clan despaired of me. But I found my way eventually. I met someone who was to change my life. He taught me so much about the world. You've," she inclined her head across the clearing to

Bobby, "got your brother, haven't you?"

Katy nodded as she leant in closer and whispered, "But he's always telling me off."

Tigress roared with laughter. "Sweetie, from what I've seen in my long life, that's the main purpose of older siblings. There was this one time in Rome when Scorp and I were tracking down this construct that had gone to ground in the Senate. We came across this senator whose brother was spending far too much time with this cheap whore…"

A deep cough resonated from Claw's side of the clearing. "Anyway, I think perhaps enough of the stories for now. We need to get going."

"Another time," the mischievous redhead mouthed to the eight-year-old, and then, out loud, "So, what's the plan, boss?"

Claw stood up, brushed himself down and reeled in his whip. "You know the drill. We inspect the ruins, find out which way the constructs went, track them down and kill them."

Chapter Three

The first thing that hit Bobby as the five of them stood at the edge of the charred ruins of his home village was the smell. When he was younger, his father had taught him that wood was a precious commodity, never to be wasted. The young Bobby would sit in his father's workshop, watching intently as the serious-faced Howard worked with sharp tools on the construction of a chair, a table or something else that he was crafting with the utmost care, and he would listen intently as the carpenter explained, "We are so used to wood being all around us. The trees beyond the village grow with no tending. They are not like the crops in our garden that need our constant attention and care. They are wild creatures that follow their own rules and will grow back time and time again as long as we only take what we need. This is abhorrent to Kanor and his soldiers. They control humans by making sure that we suffer and that we are…" pausing, he glanced at the boy with concern, "reduced in number. No matter how much they try, they cannot temper the forces of nature. They cannot fix a harness around its mouth and ride it like a tame stallion. Every so often, they will come by and torch the forests, reducing them to ash. I remember this from when I was younger than you, the Shadow Wraiths arrived with an army of those faceless beasts. They cut down the trees, stacking up kindling in the woods. Then, using pitch and flame, they burned it to the ground. Yet, within twelve months, fresh shoots were creeping up from the scorched earth. Within a year, there was wild bracken. Within two, there was a base of undergrowth. By my tenth year, young trees were once again reaching for the sky. By the time I was fifteen, we had a new, full forest ready for coppicing and trimming for wood that we could utilise once again.

"No matter what it thinks, evil will never beat back the forces of nature. However, we need to be ready for the times that it will try." He had shown Bobby how to salvage every last scrap of waste wood from his work: how to sweep the floor until every single mote of stray sawdust had been gathered; how to efficiently store every off-cut and every sliver of unused timber. "These are what we should burn for fuel," he explained, "not the prime wood that we must use to fashion those items that we need. And, as we burn it to heat our homes and to cook our food, we hope and pray that we will have enough stored and hidden for the day that those monsters return to try and impose their will upon the nature that surrounds us. For if we do not, we will be forced to eat food that is cold and tasteless and freeze to death come the long winter nights."

The smell that reached Bobby's nostrils this early evening, just after the sun had dipped down below the horizon, was akin to the aroma of the scavenged firewood that he and his father had set light to in their hearth that day, long ago. It told of wood that had blazed at incredible temperatures.

However, whereas the homely fire that he and his father had created had been intended to preserve life, the fire that had blazed in Irlingbury for the past day or so had been ignited for quite the opposite intention.

Bobby wrinkled his nose. "The smell of the burnt wood is wrong. Why is that?"

The three adults exchanged glances.

"It wasn't just wood that burned here," Claw explained in a low voice. He reached up and rubbed at the back of his neck, his hood now hanging down, as were those of the other two, between his shoulder blades. "Listen, perhaps you and Katy ought to wait here with the horses."

Bobby looked at the three horses that had been tethered to the remains of a scorched tree. The three beasts were innocently chewing at a patch of grass.

"If it's okay with you, I think I'd rather not."

"But, there will be things there you might not want to see."

Bobby thought about Katy shoving

Teller to his death from atop a stone bridge. "There are already things in my life that I wish I hadn't laid eyes upon."

Claw looked unconvinced.

"We're wasting valuable nighttime," Tigress urged. "Besides, we can't leave them here on their own. What if there are patrols or scouts?"

The man nodded in solemn acceptance. "Very well." Then, to the children, "Just, be careful."

The five of them headed into the remains of the village.

Not one building that they passed remained untouched by the devastation. As they progressed down the main road towards the centre of Irlingbury, scorched ruins flanked them on either side like a grim honour guard at a funeral procession. Acrid smoke rose from the smouldering ruins. Ash drifted lazily in the air, settling on the ground so that the floor now resembled a pale grey carpet. Bobby found himself constantly rubbing at his eyes to relieve the tears that were welling up in irritation at the intrusive dust.

"Reminds me of Pompeii," Tigress muttered, half to herself, half to Scorpion as they constantly scanned the ruins and side streets for signs of life or danger.

The blonde replied with a taciturn shrug.

"I know, I know. That actually had a purpose, whereas this…" The redhead made a noise of disgust. "Damn animated lumps of clay."

Claw just walked in silence — his brown eyes peering intently through the gathering gloom, his feet placing themselves one after the other, his tread hardly raising any ash from the dusty road.

Eventually, they reached the market square. The last time that Bobby and Katy had been here, it had been bustling, full of the villagers of Irlingbury going about their business, buying food to feed their families.

This evening, it was once more full of the villagers of the small settlement, but not one of them would be buying or selling ever again. Bobby stood numb as he tried to take in the sight that greeted him. He had witnessed death before, violent death, over the last few days, but not on this sort of scale. All around the edge of the square, bodies hung from tattered remnants of burnt-out buildings. Some bore ragged holes in what remained of their chests, testament to the death inflicted upon them by the constructs. Others were missing body parts — legs, arms, heads. All were scorched and burnt, some completely down to the bone, most to a mass of runny, gooey pulp that was sloughing from their exposed skeletons.

He tried to turn away from the sight, but whichever way he looked, the macabre horror confronted him, nauseated him. He opened his mouth to say something but, as he did, he realised that Katy was missing. His head flicked left and right as his eyes scanned the local vicinity. She was nowhere to be seen. Nowhere at all.

The three adults were standing to the side of the square discussing something. They hadn't noticed that she was gone.

Bobby did what he considered to be the right thing. He turned and ran, retracing their steps through the burnt-out village. As his feet plumed up clouds of ash, he concentrated on two things. The first was listening for the telltale *thud thud* of any approaching constructs. The last thing he needed right now was to bump into one of the monstrous killing machines. The second was studying the path in front of him. Through the grey ash on the floor, Bobby could make out scuffed footprints left by his feet. The three adults had left barely a mark. After a short while, he came across a smaller set of prints that had veered off down a side alley.

Bobby frowned. Where on earth was she going? He twisted and turned through the charred remnants of back alleys and side streets until, after a few minutes, he had a feeling of recognition, of familiarity, as he chased through the scorched remains and realised where Katy was headed.

Home.

He found his sister sitting on a large stump of a tree that their father had felled before they had both been born. It was on the edge of their property and had always been a place where they had enjoyed play-ing together. Little Katy had always giggled as she had clambered up onto the remains of the old tree and had squealed with delight as she had flung herself off into the waiting arms of her big brother. The big brother who found her now sat there, looking over the barren land where they had spent their earliest years. Her eyes were fixed on the overgrown plot of the house that had been destroyed years before the constructs had torched the rest of their village.

Her eyes snapped up towards Bobby as he gently called her name.

"Why are you here?" he asked, his eyes cautiously flicking from side to side. "It's dangerous."

"Everywhere's dangerous," she shrugged. "Why should here be any different?"

Bobby opened his mouth to answer her but found that there was nothing that he could say in reply. She had a point. He joined her on the stump and looked across the ruined patch of land. Where once crops had grown, there was wild, barbarous bracken. Where once had stood a house, there was just rough scrub, all usable materials from the demolished building having been scavenged and taken away.

"There's nothing left," the small girl finally said. "Nothing at all. Everything we ever had is gone. We are all that remains in our life now. First mum, then dad and our home, now our village. They've taken everything that was dear to us and destroyed it all, bit by bit.

"When will it all stop? *How* can it all stop?"

Bobby studied his sister's face, expecting to see sadness, tears rolling down her cheeks. What he saw, however, was much worse. There was a hardness to her young features, a cold resolve that he had witnessed once before. It was how she had looked the day that she had killed Teller.

This was not the face of a young child.

"Katy," he began, carefully searching for the right words, "we know that the world in which we live is cruel, vicious. We have seen what constructs can do and those that pay lip service to the Black Dragon. They make people suffer. They ruin lives. Yes, they have done so to us, too. But there is one thing that they have not done, that they *cannot* do."

Her small face looked up at him. "What's that?"

"They can't take you away from me. I will always be here for you and you will be here for me."

A touch of a smile curled her lips upwards and she nodded.

Bobby climbed down off the stump. "We'd better get back to the others."

As they walked away from their old life, Katy asked, "What do you think they are?"

"The others?"

She nodded. "I've never seen anyone or anything like them. They are so fast and strong. Do you think they are as old as they claim to be?"

Bobby shrugged. "I don't know. I don't see how they could be, but then I don't see why they should lie about it. They have been good to us and haven't tried to harm us, have they."

"I like them. They feel so… *confident.* It's as if they know how things truly are."

"I know what you mean. It's like when Dad used to tell us stories. We would sit there, listening to every word, wondering how it would end. Would the hero succeed? What dangers would he meet on the way? Yet, Dad obviously already knew. He had been told the same story by *his* father and he knew where it was headed, what the conclusion would be. Claw, Scorpion and Tigress are like that. They've already been told the story, but rather than telling it to someone else, they are living it out in their own lives."

"I think that's great!" Katy grinned. "Imagine how it must be, knowing how something was already going to end. I'd like that. I'd like that *a lot*."

As the two of them traipsed through the mud and the ash, Bobby pondered this. What would it be like to know the path that your life was going to take? Sure, it could be useful. You could plan ahead for certain things, be forewarned. However, surely the ending would always be the same, no matter what twists or turns the story took? Imagine living with that constantly digging away in the back of your head.

He decided that he would not like it. Not

one little bit.

It was as they turned a corner onto the main road back into the village that they heard it. At first, it did not fully register. It was just another background noise, a monotonous beat that may have been just something or nothing. But then, as it drew closer, it became dreadfully apparent that this was not something from the day-to-day, something from the mundane.

Besides, in a village where all the inhabitants were dead, how could anything alive be moving?

Thud, thud. Thud, thud.

Making their way down the ash-strewn road, Katy and Bobby felt the vibration of the construct's leaden feet before they saw the clay monster itself. The heavy pulse travelled up through the mud and the ash, along the muscles of their legs and into their stomachs, where it gripped their innards tight and squeezed.

They turned as one and watched the clay giant lumber slowly around a corner. Its slick skin glistened eerily in the rising light of the pale moon, casting a dull shadow on the path behind it.

It did not pause.

It did not falter.

It did not stop to observe its prey.

It just continued walking. Straight towards them.

"Run!" Bobby screamed, and the two of them turned tail and fled. "This way!" Bobby jerked his sister down a small alley, almost yanking her small arm out of her shoulder socket. "Follow me." He leapt across the collapsed timbers of what used to be a doorway into a small house. Katy scrambled across in his wake. The teenage boy hoped that the fallen debris would provide some sort of barricade or obstacle that might slow down the construct. They scurried across to the far side of the abandoned building and clambered up the ruined walls, gaining as much height as they could in an attempt to escape the soulless predator that pursued them.

As they pulled themselves out of the ruin and over into the next building, there was a deafening crash from behind them.

Bobby glanced back and felt all blood drain from his face. The construct had stretched out one of its malleable arms, wrapped them around the fallen debris in the collapsed doorway and had just yanked it out of the way as a child would throw a twig into a stream. Its thick, black tongue flicked out from the ragged gash across its otherwise featureless face as it scented the air. It calculated its new heading, turned and continued in its pursuit.

Bobby grabbed Katy's hand and pulled her down into the next building. They jumped and landed with a clatter. Knowing that to pause and check themselves over would be certain death, they ignored any scrapes and bumps that they may have sustained and fled to the other side of the burnt ruins, climbing through the remnant of the wall into an adjacent room.

There was the unmistakable sound of the construct transforming its limbs again, like that of something being pulled out of wet, sticky mud. As Bobby and Katy turned a corner that led them back out into the street, they caught sight of the monster descending into the room into which they had jumped. It had stretched its legs out like gigantic stilts and was stepping with apparent ease from the top of one building down into the room of the next. As it touched down on the floor, each leg shrunk back into its body and not once did it break step, its pursuit unencumbered, relentless.

The children scrabbled their way through a broken doorway and hurtled out into the dead street. Behind them the steady, unstoppable pace of the construct continued to haunt their ears. In his terrified mind, Bobby kept expecting to hear the creature's body transform one more time and for him to feel a sudden jab of excruciating pain and look down at the tip of a lance jutting through his chest, just as Rose had done when she had given her life to save Katy.

He shook his head.

There could be no thoughts like that; they were a distraction that he could not afford. They just had to keep on running. They slid and skidded in the loose ash as they careened around a corner back onto the main street that led down towards the market square. The two children pumped their arms as they hurtled down the abandoned street, ash and dust pluming up from under their feet that slapped frantically on the rutted surface. Bobby's lungs began to burn from the continued exertion as they rushed past more burnt-out ruins before careering into the opening of the market square. They looked around for the three adults but saw just the dead remnants of the villagers of Irlingbury.

All the time behind them came the relentless, non-stop drum of the construct's march.

Thud, thud. Thud, thud.

Panicked, their hearts ready to burst from their chests, the two children searched for somewhere to hide — somewhere dark and small in which they could cower like a tiny rodent that wishes to escape the attention of the housewife chasing it with a broom. But there was nowhere, nothing. All the once-thriving marketplace could provide them with was the constant demonstration that a brutal death awaited them. The dead hung everywhere, choking the life from every corner.

And soon, Bobby and Katy were to join them.

Bobby flung his arms around his kid sister and dragged her eyes away from the sight of the construct marching unimpeded into the open. There was nothing more that they could do. They were exhausted, all the energy in their young bodies consumed, whereas the creature of clay had no such handicap. Bobby covered Katy's ears as the construct stretched out its arm, the trans-formation of the limb into a cruel lance ac-companied by the all too familiar sound that was akin to wet mud.

It continued, unbothered, towards the two children.

Katy writhed in her brother's grip and tore her face away from his chest. She pushed at her stunned sibling, stepped to-wards the towering golem and screamed in unintelligible rage at the creature that's only concern was her imminent and brutal death.

Bobby shook his head and made to grab her, to preserve even the slightest fraction of a second more of her life, but she just shoved him away and continued to scream at the clay monster as it bore down upon her.

And then, sprinting out of the shadows, a dark blur crashed into the side of the construct at such a velocity, that it sent the killer cartwheeling head over heels across the market square, causing it to crash into the charred remains of a former building. Two more shapes, moving faster than the mortal brain could understand, joined with the first and the three of them seemed to pick the construct up from the ground and hurl it back across to the other side of the marketplace. It collided with a sickening *crump* into a heap of discarded bodies. Bobby watched in awe as the monster made to lift itself to its feet only to stumble and fall once more as a black whip cracked out across the night and lashed around its left leg. The construct tried yet again to walk but Claw pulled tight, yanking the whip high over his shoulder and the creature fell once more.

This time, Tigress and Scorpion leapt and landed on its arms, pinning them to the ground.

The construct made to struggle, but the grip of the two women was unbreakable. Their pale hands held it fast to the floor as Claw approached the fallen golem, keeping a tight rein on his whip as he did so. Then Bobby gasped in shock as sharp points thrust out from the construct's chest, jabbing upwards towards its captors in a desperate bid to harpoon them. But the women were too quick and, each time an improvised weapon lunged up towards them, they seemed to nimbly edge out of the way as if they had not been in its path at all.

Bobby continued to watch as the women glanced at each other before opening their mouths wide. What the boy saw chilled him almost as much as the monster itself. At the edge of their lips, they both bore a sharp pair of fangs that glinted in the moonlight, wet with their hungry saliva. In unison the two women plunged their sharpened teeth down into the material of the construct's arms and to Bobby's revulsion, they appeared to drink.

The construct writhed and flailed under

them, a deep wail emanating from its wide mouth as its black tongue whipped back and forth.

It was in utter agony.

Never before had Bobby seen the like.

"Enough!" Claw's voice was sharp and commanding across the howls of terror from the dying creature. "We need it alive."

The two women raised their heads and glared at the male as he untied his whip from the creature's leg. Ignoring their annoyance, he took the tip of his weapon, the silver barb, raised it high then plunged it down into the chest of the construct. The monster shrieked in a high-pitched wail that turned Bobby's stomach over in his guts. He looked on in morbid fascination as the construct seemed to shake and convulse as Claw rammed his hand in after the tip of the whip, stern concentration on his face as he twisted the barb around inside his prisoner's flailing body.

Then, the impossible happened.

In front of Bobby's eyes, the construct's skin shifted and melted. The huge clay beast was no more and there, trapped by the three captors lay what appeared to be a naked human woman.

"Let me go! Let me go!" the woman screamed, her head flailing from side to side. "Let me go!"

"Not going to happen." Claw's voice was calm and commanding. "You're going to tell us what we want to know."

"Go to hell, *vampire!*" she hissed. "Why should I tell you anything, you weak abomination? You're a pathetic little remnant and your days are numbered."

"Says the lump of clay with a claw in its chest." He twisted his wrist as a painful reminder of the fact.

The woman's agonised screams echoed around the market square.

"Who ordered this? Who said the village was to be destroyed?"

The prisoner gritted her teeth, seeming to muster up all her strength, then glaring at Claw's passive face, she hissed, "Why should I tell you anything? You are weak, pathetic. You couldn't even destroy the Bloodline of Abel. No, the mighty Children of Cain had to depend on a mere mortal to do their dirty work for them. Thousands of years and you did nothing, just lurking, brooding in the shadows and how long did it take him to eradicate the Bloodline from the face of the planet? A few months?" She slammed the back of her head against the cobbled floor and brayed in laughter. "Pathetic! Totally pathetic."

"Tell me," Claw persevered, "who ordered the destruction of the village, and why?"

The woman's eyes burnt with fire as she glared up at him, ignoring the questions. "Tell me, *vampire*, where is he now, your great saviour? Where is Sam Spallucci? He's nowhere! He's gone, never to return. He's..." Her words cut out as she opened her mouth as wide as possible and screamed in agony.

Bobby's hand flew to his mouth as he watched Tigress wipe a knife against the skin of the woman, just above where she had severed the prisoner's foot from her leg. "You want to lose another one? Because I'm game. Answer the questions."

"Never," the woman spat through

clenched teeth as she tried to control her breathing. "I'll never betray him."

Claw raised an eyebrow. "Which *him*?"

"Screw you!"

Claw nodded to Tigress.

The woman screamed again as, this time, she lost a hand.

Bobby watched in morbid fascination as both the foot and the hand began to grow back, plain stumps edging out from the traumatised limbs, stretching and expanding to fill the spaces that the foot and the hand had previously occupied.

Claw sighed and bent down to the face of the woman. "You know we can do this all night. We just cut things off and wait for them to grow back. Eventually, you will tire. Eventually, you will tell me what I want to know."

In total, the woman lost six feet, seven hands and a nose before she finally cracked.

"Asmodeus!" she wept. "It was Asmodeus. The Fallen gave the order."

"Why?"

She shook her head. "I don't know. He

was angry. So angry. I think he had received a roasting from *higher up*."

The three vampires glanced at each other.

"Where is he now? How many con-structs does he have with him?"

"He's not far. He's to the north, camped on the Rishton wetlands. He has about ten constructs." She closed her eyes and her head sank exhausted to the floor. It was a look of utter, total defeat.

Claw studied the woman's sunken face for a moment before nodding to his two companions. Scorpion and Tigress once more revealed their fangs and bit down hard on the woman's wrists. This time she only managed a feeble moan as they drank heavily from her.

In a short while, she was nothing but fine, powdery dust.

Chapter Four

They climbed on their horses and left the smouldering ruins of Irlingbury behind them as they rode out into the night. Not pushing their steeds, they proceeded cautiously along the old road which led north out of the village.

In an hour or so, they reined in outside a curious looking building. Unlike most other structures that Bobby and Katy had known, it was constructed from stone, not wood, and rather than composing of the usual four walls, it had just three, its base forming that of a triangle.

But, perhaps more unusual than anything else, it was almost perfectly intact.

Claw dismounted and walked up to the door of the building. He turned the large iron handle and, with a small amount of effort, it opened inwards. "We will rest here," he said. The other vampires climbed down from their horses, helping the children to dismount.

As the adults settled the horses and took supplies into the building, Bobby wandered around the other side of the structure whilst Katy followed after Tigress and Scorpion. He gazed up in wonder at the design of the building that appeared incredibly old but was in unbelievably good condition. Everywhere he looked there was threefold symbolism. The building had three straight sides and he noted that there were three floors. Not only that, but most of the windows were fashioned from patterns of triangles. He walked back towards the main door and saw writing across the top of the stone lintel. He frowned, unable to read it.

"*Tres testimonium dant,*" came a gnarled, familiar voice from behind him.

Bobby spun around and smiled to see the old man Cutter stood there, leaning on his staff.

Bobby made to call out to him but the elderly man raised a finger to his lips. "Not here," he whispered and he motioned that they should walk a short way to a thicket of undergrowth that hid them from the sight of the building.

"It's good to see you," Bobby smiled. "Shall I get Katy?"

The man shook his head, peering cautiously across the boy's shoulder. "No, there isn't time. I can't stay long."

Bobby felt disappointed. "Oh," he managed. Then, pointing to the building, he said, "It's quite amazing, isn't it? How come it's survived this long?"

"It is the symbolism of the place. The notion of three appeals to Kanor. Its original architect would have meant it to stand for something else, a long-dead religious belief, but to Kanor it means something completely different."

"That inscription. What does it mean?"

"*There are three that give witness.*"

Bobby frowned. "And what does *that* mean?"

"Probably not what it was originally intended to. Possibly more than the soul who inscribed it could have fathomed." Cutter paused, his sharp eyes studying Bobby. "Are you well? I saw what happened to Irlingbury."

Bobby silently nodded, not wanting to talk about what they had seen.

Cutter tutted appreciatively. "Listen and listen well. You are in danger. You and Katy need to be extremely careful."

Bobby turned and frowned at the triangular building. "It doesn't appear dangerous. It seems quite solid."

Cutter shook his head. "I do not mean the structure; I mean those within it. You cannot trust the Children of Cain. They are ruthless killers and will draw you into their righteous war. You must not fight their battles. It will be the death of you."

Bobby made to ask what he meant exactly, when there was a noise. He glanced across to the building and saw Claw approaching. Turning back, he found that Cutter had slipped away into the darkness of the night.

"Are you okay?" the sandy-haired man called. "I thought I heard voices."

"Just talking to myself," Bobby

shrugged as nonchalantly as he could.

Claw paused and Bobby watched as the adult sniffed the air before frowning in apparent puzzlement

"Come on. We've made some food. You'd better grab some before your sister eats the lot."

The night was starting to fade away as the five travellers rested in the curious triangular building. The two children ate as the three adults checked over their gear. Bobby watched the three intently as they went about their own individual chores.

Claw inspected every part of his long whip: pulling it taut between his pale hands to test its strength, examining the sharp metal talon at the end that he had plunged into the chest of the construct. Using a smooth cloth that he kept on his person, he polished it until its silvery surface glinted in the light of the small campfire that they had set in the room's hearth.

Tigress appeared to be carrying more knives than seemed physically possible. She pulled them out from concealed slots and pockets in her clothes, lying them out in front of her in three neat rows, before meticulously cleaning each one and running a sharpening steel over their already finely honed blades.

Scorpion sat with her back to the wall of the weirdly shaped room and just stared straight ahead into the fire. Unlike the other two, who were concentrating on matters of the here and now, she seemed to be far off in some other place. Her eyes danced with firelight as she sat motionless, as still as a corpse.

Cutter had insisted that these three individuals were dangerous. Yet twice now they had saved Bobby's and Katy's lives. The old man had never been wrong before, acting as some sort of gnarled guardian angel, yet how could these three bear them harm?

But then, he and Katy knew next to nothing about their apparent saviours.

About the same amount as we know about Cutter. Bobby pondered. It had been so much simpler when it had just been the two of them.

Katy finished off some cooked meat and let loose a huge belch.

The silent Scorpion cracked a slight smile and her partner slapped her thigh in amusement.

"I take it that met your satisfaction?" Claw asked as he twisted his whip into a tight coil.

Katy nodded, then frowned. "I have a question."

The three adults flicked a glance between themselves. Claw nodded for her to continue.

"The construct you killed. It called you vampires. What's one of those?"

Another look was exchanged. Scorpion tendered a small shrug, Tigress held out a hand towards Claw. "Take it away, Your Majesty," she grinned. "This is above my pay grade."

Claw seemed to blow out a puff of air as he considered what his reply should be. "As we have already said, we are all very old. Some of us," he winked at Tigress, "more so than others."

"Still feel like a hot young thing," the

redhead jibed back.

Claw chuckled and continued. "We all used to be human."

"But you're not now?" Bobby asked.

Claw shook his head. "No. We may *look* human, but we were born to a new life. A life that gives us greater strength and abilities that would be impossible for a human. We do not age as humans do. Only a handful of things can kill us: decapitation, trauma to our hearts, fire and daylight. Hence these," he explained, picking at the edge of his dark cloak. "We were all made vampires by another vampire. They did this by sharing their blood with us. So, Tigress shared the blood of her father. Scorpion shared the blood of her mother."

Tigress stuck her hand up. "Which would be me."

"And I took the blood of *my* mother."

"Where are your and Tigress' parents now?" Katy asked.

"They are dead. They have both been dead for a very long time."

The small girl frowned in thought. "Was your mother a queen? Our dad used to tell stories about kings and queens of old. They were called Your Majesty. Tigress called you that, so you must be a king, which means your mother must have been a queen."

Claw's eyes seemed incredibly sad for a moment before he continued. "Yes, she was and yes, I am."

"What was she like?"

"She was very kind. She cared for all of us. She was terribly, terribly brave."

"What did she look like?"

Claw dug deep into a pocket and pulled something out. "Here," he said, "look at this."

Katy and Bobby edged over to the vampire and peered down at the thing that he held. "What is it?" Bobby inquired.

"It is a photograph. Back when the world was as it was, people used small machines to capture the likenesses of objects and people. You see there, on the edge of the group? That is my mother."

"She looks pretty," Katy smiled. "What was her name?"

"Nightingale."

Bobby continued to study the photograph. It showed a group of people wearing fancy-looking clothes standing around some sort of stone structure, a type of large basin on a pedestal. Around the rim of the bowl were engraved five words. "*Knaves are not our responsibility*," he read. "What does that mean?"

"A whole heap of trouble," Tigress muttered as she balanced one of her knives on a fingertip.

Bobby peered back down at the photograph and frowned.

"What is it?" Claw asked.

The teenager pointed to two individuals who were standing next to the large bowl, a man in black and a boy who appeared a few years older than himself. "Who are these? They look different to the others."

An awkward silence fell across the room.

"They are of no importance right now," Claw mumbled as he tucked the photo back into his pocket. "That was a very long time ago."

"Do *you* have a child?" Katy asked.

Claw shook his head. "No. I have never taken a child. We are all that remains of our kind, the Children of Cain."

Bobby's heartbeat flickered upon his ears hearing the phrase that Cutter had used.

"Why?" Katy asked in response to Claw's answer.

The male vampire appeared to sigh. "The first vampire, Cain, was created thousands of years ago. He was given three tasks to perform, three duties to follow."

"Find the Eternals. Protect the Twins. Await the Divergence!" Tigress spat with venom in her voice. "And we sucked at all three. The Divergence came and wiped out humanity. We only found one of the Eternals. We lost the damned Twins." Bobby noticed her eyes lance Claw as she said this.

"We've been over this before…"

"Yeah, and it still sucks! Probably the greatest weapon we had to destroy Kanor and you threw it away!"

"Tigress," Claw's voice was tired, strained, as if he was sick of defending himself. "You know it was the right thing to do."

The redhead shot a word at her king in a language that the children did not understand before continuing her rant. "You sent them here, to this gods forsaken place on the basis of a dream. A dream!"

Bobby noticed Scorpion shift uncomfortably where she sat.

"You know what Scorpion saw. We had to act on it."

"Yeah, yeah, yeah. Spallucci. She saw Spallucci stood in a barren, scorched world."

"It was here. You know it was."

"For all I know it could have been the juice of a construct tripping balls on LSD! The fact remains you sent our only weapon to gods know where, leaving us utterly defenceless."

Claw shook his head. "We don't know that's what they are. They could be intended for something else entirely."

"Like what? Baking cakes?" Tigress let out a screech of frustration and hurled a knife so that it struck a wooden beam across the doorway. She shook her head. "And as for the Eternals… Gods alone know where they are now."

Claw stared resolutely into the fire. "We did what we could, but everything was stacked against us. Without knowing it, we were a hidden weakness of the very thing we were supposed to protect: humanity. We fought quietly for them in the shadows, combatting constructs and other threats when we found them. Humankind had no idea that we existed. Then, when Kanor rose and brought about the Divergence…" He shook his head despondently. "They were… unprepared."

The five sat and watched the fire crackle in its hearth, each seeing something different in their own mind.

"I want to be a vampire."

Four sets of eyes turned to the small eight-year-old girl.

"I want your strength, your speed, your abilities. I could use them to change things. I would train to be the strongest vampire ever and I would go to Wellington and kill Kanor. I would make him suffer for what he's done to everyone. I would make the world right again."

Claw shook his head. "That cannot be."

"Why not?" she protested.

He ran a hand through his sandy hair

before saying, "There was a story from my youth that told of a land a long time ago and far, far away, where a group of heroes, knights you might say, cared for society and righted all its wrongs. But they didn't know that their leader was, in reality, their greatest enemy. He created a huge army that fought alongside the knights in a terrible war, serving alongside them as brothers-in-arms. Then, on his order, that army turned and eradicated almost all those heroes who had pledged their lives to serve the weak of society. In an instant, they were but a pitiful remnant."

"That's awful," Bobby said.

Claw shook his head. "But that was not all." He looked straight at Katy. "There was one of these heroes who thought like you do Katy, that he alone knew what needed to be done, that he should gather so much power to make himself invincible to protect those that he loved."

"What happened?" the small girl asked, her eyes wide in the firelight.

"The greatest tragedy possible. The power corrupted him, blinded his conscience to darker and darker deeds that he began to undertake in the name of protecting the weak. He killed the one that he loved, betrayed his best friend. He…" Claw shook his head and Bobby was sure that the vampire wiped a red-stained tear away from his cheek. "He even slaughtered all the youngsters who were training to follow in the footsteps of the older protectors of the peace. Children, Katy, that were younger than you. He…"

"Oh, in the name of the gods!" Tigress exploded. "Seriously? You do realise that you are just describing the plot of *Revenge of the Sith*?"

A certain awkwardness fell across Claw's face. "Well, it does have an unusual parallel with our situation. I feel it has a strong moral that we can take away and…"

The redhead snorted in derision. "Idiot!" she snapped as she threw a stone on the fire, causing hot embers to dance up into the air. "Here we sit in a post-apocalyptic wilderness which hasn't even known proper sanitation for over a thousand years, let alone electricity, and you tell these baffled kids about a film from your childhood! Unbe-lievable. No wonder they wiped us out!"

"It's a very relevant story," Claw tried to explain.

"It's a complete fiction!" Tigress screamed at him. "Just like the idea that there is some honest soul out there that will take out Kanor and make this all right again."

"The Virtuous Man exists," Claw stated plainly.

"You mean Jason? From Orchester?"

Claw turned to Bobby and shook his head. "There was not a grain of virtue in that man's body. He was a fraud that had tricked even himself into believing the lie. The real Virtuous Man is still out there, somewhere."

"Oh, gods," Tigress moaned. "Here we go again. The bromance to end all bromances!"

Scorpion got up and gestured for her to calm down.

"No! No, I will not! It is a fool's errand. There is no Virtuous Man!"

The blonde set her fists on her hips and glared at the redhead.

"Yes, yes! I know. The *prophecies.* The damned prophecies. A fat lot of good they've done so far."

"He's out there," Claw insisted. "We will find him."

"No. We won't. Spallucci is dead. You hear me? He's dead. He died the day the bombs went off. Before Lucifer and Abaddon…"

"No!" Claw had sprung to his feet, flown across the room and now had Tigress pinned by her throat against the stone wall. "He is alive! I know it. I feel it. We will find him and he will save us!"

Bobby protectively drew Katy towards him but she shrugged him off once more.

Scorpion forced herself between the two arguing vampires and thrust them apart before glowering at each of them in turn. The pair sat down, both of them staring at the floor in disgrace. The blonde shook her head in frustration and came over to the siblings. Crouching down, she placed a cold hand on each of them and cocked her head in a question.

"It's okay," Katy smiled, "we argue too."

Scorpion nodded, turned to look at the others, and sighed.

Chapter Five

They arrived at the wetlands of Rishton just before nightfall. It had been a very tense ride north with the three vampires saying very little to each other following their spat at the triangular tower. Scorpion was her usual taciturn self and the atmosphere between Claw and Tigress was practically tangible. The only real conversation had been when the children had watched a tall structure rise on the horizon to the west.

"What's that?" Bobby asked pointing across the flatlands to the thin shape that seemed to dart its way up to the sky. "It's so tall."

"That," Claw said without even troubling to glance at the building in the distance, "is Wellington. That is somewhere you never wish to go, you hear?"

"Why not?"

"The tall building you see used to be a church, where people used to pray to their god."

"Jason mentioned something about that. He said he was a priest."

Claw made a small annoyed tutting noise. "That man's god would be ashamed of him for what he did to you."

"So why should we not go to that place then? Are there more there like Jason?"

"No," Claw explained, guiding his horse away from the settlement. "It is now the lair of Kanor. If you were to go there, you would die."

As they continued north, Bobby watched the spire fade into the darkening landscape and, as the sun sank down behind its imposing silhouette, he imagined that he could see a huge pair of black wings rising from the descending fiery ball up into the night sky.

Nothing else was said until the vampires drew their horses to a stop. They settled their rides by a small stand of trees that grew next to a wide plain of lush grass. It appeared a richer shade of green than anywhere else that Bobby had ever seen. Tigress caught him staring out across the wide landscape. "There's a lot of water here under the surface. It's something to do with the ground below. It enables the grass to grow easier than in most places. Look." She dismounted her steed, walked over to a patch of grass and placed her foot upon it. A pool of water pushed up the sides of her boot.

"Is it safe to walk on?" Bobby asked.

"I would advise against you going out there. You could hit a soft patch and sink below the surface. We, on the other hand, are far more agile and can just bounce around like dandelion heads in the wind," she grinned. "Ones with very sharp teeth, that is."

Katy came and stood next to them, wrinkling her nose. "It smells awful."

"The water is stagnant," Tigress explained. "It can't flow so it just sits here and smells bad."

Bobby nodded.

"Where are the constructs?"

As one, the vampires peered out across the wetlands. They all nodded and Claw said, "They are due north, across the marshland. We can make out their encampment over on the other side. It's a good job we can see where they are as we can't smell them across this quagmire."

"Smell them?"

The vampire nodded. "It is one of our skills. It helps us hunt them, even when they are not in their natural form."

"Like the one at Irlingbury?"

"Back before the Divergence, that was how most of them were. They looked like you, me, your sister and they walked freely among society. Most of them didn't even know what they were until something triggered them. Then they would turn on families, friends, co-workers." He shook his head. "There were a few ways to discern them, but their scent was always unmistakable."

"They smell almost as bad as this foetid water," Tigress chipped in. "Totally unnatural, unhealthy. They could mask it with scent or use other techniques such as staying dirty and unwashed, but we usually got them in the end.

"Until there were too many of them."

A sombre silence fell upon the group, which was finally broken by Claw. "Well, that won't be an issue tonight. Ten is a nice easy number, I think we can all agree."

The two female vampires nodded. "A walk in the park. What's the plan of attack, boss?" Tigress asked.

Claw unhooked his whip from his belt and began flexing the long weapon as he pondered their strategy. "I say a pincer manoeuvre. I'll come at them from the left, you two from the right.

"But Asmodeus is mine. Remember that."

The two other vampires nodded. "Goes without saying," Tigress nodded.

Bobby saw the look of determination mixed with anger that fell across Claw's face. "What is it with Asmodeus?"

"It's revenge, pure and simple. He killed my mother."

Bobby didn't know what to say. Claw

had said that his mother was dead, but the fact that the person who had been responsible for her death was so close… Finally, he asked. "The construct said that he was one of the Fallen. Who exactly is he?"

Starting to check over her knives, Tigress muttered, "He's a jerk."

"He's also incredibly dangerous," Claw warned. "The Fallen, there are two of them: Asmodeus, the male, and Asherah, the female. They are, or *were*, angels. They are both older than this planet and used to live in a realm called Heaven until they became restless and greedy, then they fell to Earth, where they have been ever since."

"With massive chips on their shoulders," Tigress interjected.

Bobby frowned. He didn't have any idea as to what she meant. "Are they powerful?"

Claw nodded. "Amongst other things, they can control elements. Asherah can draw water from the air around her and use it as a tool or a weapon. Asmodeus can produce lightning from his fingers. If he fires it at your kind, it would be excruciatingly painful or indeed deadly. We can tolerate it better than you can."

"Oh, I'm not so sure about that," came a smooth voice from behind them. "My master is always happy to prove a Child of Cain wrong." A Shadow Wraith emerged from the trees. Following him were four constructs.

The vampires moved without hesitation. Any differences they might have been arguing over were discarded, forgotten as they attacked like a well maintained, regularly oiled weapon. Even before Bobby could blink, three of the constructs were suddenly lying on the floor, their legs amputated at the knees. Tigress was circling back around on them, a stout blade in her hand. As she advanced on the first, Scorpion had slid between the legs of the one that remained standing, levering herself upright, causing it too to fall to the floor before she latched down on its clay skin with her sharp teeth, her body moving fluidly from side to side to avoid the sharp lances that the downed construct shot up from its torso in a vain attempt to skewer her. Shortly, two constructs were nothing but powdery dust and the two females were draining the other two.

There was a loud crack as Claw flicked his whip out and coiled the end around the Shadow Wraith's neck. He yanked backwards, trying to pull the creature off its feet, but the Wraith moved with the motion of the whip and sailed through the air, landing lithely behind the vampire. With its pale hands, it gripped the taut cord and jerked it down, continuing to work with the momentum of the weapon. Claw staggered and almost lost his grip, but he became a blur and, in less than a second, the Wraith was trussed tight in the whip that was now snaked around his body. It began to writhe against the bonds, its skin taking on a softer, more viscous hue, but Claw screamed out in rage and effort as he pulled the weapon to its tightest. The Shadow Wraith seemed to lose its solid consistency and partially oozed through the coiled weapon. Claw reached under his cloak and, in one swift movement, produced a wicked-looking knife that he swung through the neck of the Wraith, causing its head to tumble to the floor, its eyes staring up in horrified shock. The vampire launched onto the decapitated body, sunk his teeth into the exposed neck and sucked loudly as the body withered and desiccated.

In less than a hundred heartbeats, the three vampires were stood over the remains of the dead creatures. Bobby realised that he could not recall having breathed during the whole process. He turned to look at Katy. The eight-year-old was stood enrapt, a broad smile filling her face.

"That was *amazing*," she breathed.

"It's what we do," Tigress winked. Then, to Claw, "A trap?"

"Definitely," he agreed, then turned and gazed out across the wetlands, an odd look on his face.

"What is it?" the redhead asked.

Claw frowned. "I'm not sure. I'm sure I have a memory of this place from a long, long time ago. But, so much has happened since. It's just a vague image of fighting." He shook his head. "Forget it." Then, to the other two vampires, "So, they knew we were coming. You want to pull back?"

The redhead glanced at her blonde partner who was staring out across the marshland, her sharp teeth still exposed. "Like hell we do," Tigress snarled.

Claw smiled and nodded. "My thoughts exactly. Bobby, you and Katy must stay here, you understand? Whatever you see or hear, you do not intervene. If you do, you will die."

Katy made to open her mouth but the vampire held up a silencing hand. "No. On no account do you set one foot on that marshland. You remain here and await our return. If we don't come back, then you run. You run for your lives. Do I make myself clear?"

The children nodded.

He turned to the other vampires. "Asmodeus is out there. We know what he did. Let's make him pay," and they set out across the open marsh.

Even with the knowledge that they were walking into a trap, the vampires stuck to their original plan, feeling that it was the most practical tactic. Claw circled left, his hood back and his taloned whip in his hand. His dark eyes were black against his pale skin in the cold moonlight. They flicked back and forth intent, waiting for the trap to be sprung. Every now and then his head tilted to one side, then the other, his eyes carefully regarding the wet ground upon which he lightly trod. Tigress and Scorpion progressed right, around the other side of the marshland. They walked side by side, a watchful confidence apparent about them. In her hands, Tigress carried two of her wicked-looking knives, their finely honed edges glinting delicately in the light of the crescent moon. Scorpion held a short sword down by her side. It looked like she was holding it loose, casually, but Bobby knew that was not the case. The blonde, like the other woman, was a trained killing machine. Her sharp blade would be thrusting, slicing, killing as soon as they came under attack.

As they did roughly halfway across the open marshland.

One moment, the vampires were stalking their way carefully across the wet surface of the land, the next they had frozen solid, aware of something that was beyond the mortal senses of Bobby and Katy.

Then the ground around the vampires began to move.

The surface of the marsh started to undulate as if it were being breathed upon by some unseen deity. Ripples radiated out from points all around the vampires and Bobby's jaw fell slack as he witnessed the rise of not ten, not twenty, but thirty constructs from the depths of the marsh.

It was like watching an army of tree trunks emerge slowly in unison from the ground. First there was the dome of the top of their heads, then the broad shoulders, followed by the rest of their bodies, including the long, deadly arms with cruel lances protruding from the end of the limbs.

The three vampires did not hesitate. As one blur of motion, they struck whilst the constructs were still sprouting from the wet marsh. They managed to dispatch half a dozen before they had fully formed.

But that still left them terribly outnumbered and they were now fighting for their lives.

They had speed on their side as the constructs were heavy, cumbersome creatures and struggled to march to their usual steady beat through the dank watery surface. Tigress and Scorpion lithely lifted themselves off from the ground and catapulted across the heads of the golems, slashing and skewering with their blades as they did. The children watched as, at one point, the blonde vampire used five constructs as if they were steppingstones, slicing down beneath her as she travelled across them, deftly dodging side to side, outmanoeuvring their thrusting lances.

But slicing and incapacitating the creatures was only half the battle. If the vampires did not drain them, they just drew themselves together and reformed, reentering the fray with their unrelenting steady pace.

The two females adapted their battle plan accordingly. Scorpion continued to slice the clay monsters apart, causing them to fall to the wet surface of the marsh, allowing Tigress to latch on to the severed remains and quickly drain them dry.

It was a shrewd tactic but, as Bobby watched powerlessly from the side, he could not help but feel that the women were fighting a losing battle. As Tigress continued to drain construct after construct, Scorpion seemed to be slaying one after another quicker than her partner could finish them off. This meant that, in the intervening time between slash and despatch, a number of the golems were able to reform and reenter the battle. As a result, the number of constructs that Scorpion actually had to fight kept increasing, which meant one worrying thing.

She was getting noticeably tired.

Claw also had a Battle Royale on his hands. He was taking a different tactic, having to fight through swathes of oncoming constructs on his own as he ploughed his way towards his Ultima Thule, the revenge for the death of his mother. Streaking up the lefthand side of the battlefield, his whip continually cracked out across the fray, parting one construct after another from its head. However, rather than staying to finish the jobs, the male vampire had another target in sight.

Bobby peered across to the far side of

the carnage where he saw two figures standing side by side. One with its smooth white hair was undoubtedly a Shadow Wraith. The other was a figure that he did not recognise. It was male, of apparently average height, and wore a flowing black cloak over its shoulders.

"Asmodeus!" Claw screamed as he ran towards the two figures. "I have come for you!"

The Fallen said something to the Shadow Wraith and the slick killing machine at once darted across the wetland towards the raging vampire. The construct flicked out its arms and they formed into two savage curved blades which it swung at Claw as it leapt across the ground towards him. The vampire met the creature mid-air and they collided with a furious impact, causing both parties to crash to the floor. The construct came up first, raising its blade hands, preparing to thrust them into its downed enemy. However, its grin of malice vanished as a sharp crack echoed across the battlefield and the hook from Claw's whip dug into the side of its head. The vampire jerked his weapon to the right and the creature's head ripped across the middle as Claw bounced to his feet. In one fluid movement, he had pushed the severed form of the Shadow Wraith to the floor and had sunk his teeth into its clay flesh. When he raised his face from transforming the construct into powder, he turned to confront his nemesis.

That was when the battlefield was lit up with the crackling devastation of Asmodeus' lightning.

Bobby screamed out as Claw was lifted from his feet and dangled like a stringless marionette amongst the deadly electricity that poured out of the fingers of his nemesis. The Fallen advanced towards the helpless vampire, a cruel grin on his sallow features. He pulled his hands back, briefly relenting his barrage and allowing the vampire to crash limply to the floor. Then, when he was sure that the vampire would not rise to attack him, he resumed his assault, bright lightning crackling across the stricken victim, smoke rising from the vampire's singed clothing.

Bobby shook his head. This couldn't be

happening. The Children of Cain were unlike any folk he had ever known. They were sharp, deadly, unbeatable, yet here they were, overwhelmed and failing. His eyes flicked back and forth from Claw being assailed over and over by the relentless lightning of the gleeful Asmodeus to the pair of Scorpion and Tigress as they doggedly took out construct after construct at a slower and slower pace.

Then he looked to his side, to his kid sister.

Who wasn't there.

"Katy! Katy!" he screamed, his head turning this way and that, desperate to locate his only living relative. Then he spied her. She was dodging across the battlefield, taking a circuitous route around the melee towards the fallen Claw. Bobby felt his stomach lurch and his skin pale as he couldn't believe his eyes.

There was only one thing he could do.

He followed her onto the battlefield.

The route across the marshland was treacherous. Bobby stumbled and fell to his knees several of times, swallowing mouthfuls of vile stagnant water, but he heaved himself up and continued to chase after his lighter, more nimble kid sister as she pelted hell for leather towards the light-show of Asmodeus torturing the prone vampire.

Fortunately, like the vampires, the children had agility on their side and were able to dance around the side of any constructs that stumbled and lurched at them through the clinging mire of the marshland. Twice Bobby had to roll to one side to avoid a thrusting lance, but he left the constructs behind him, concentrating on one thing and one thing alone, reaching his sister. He tried to cry out after her, but his limbs ached and his lungs burned. All his energy was being used to propel his legs on through the deepening, grasping quagmire. As Bobby felt his last reserves drive him onwards, he grasped at mud and clay as he watched Katy sprint across the final distance of the battlefield towards the lifeless form of Claw. He pulled himself towards his sister as he heard her scream at the Fallen in unintelligible rage. Asmodeus paused in his assault on his old enemy and turned his attention to the new-comer. His brow frowned and his eyebrow rose in amusement. Bobby watched in horror as the Fallen drew back his hand, electricity beginning to dance across his fingers. However, a black shadow fell across the would-be child killer as Claw summoned up the last of his failing strength to heave himself up and catapult his weakened body into the Fallen.

The two of them crashed into the mud.

Asmodeus was the first to regain his feet. A mask of entire fury consumed his face and he made to strike the final blow.

Bobby forced himself forward, pushing his feet in the marsh with all the remaining strength that he could muster and threw himself across the last remaining distance, ending up across the fallen form of Claw. He looked up into the face of Asmodeus and watched the electricity build and crackle.

And then there was nothing.

The assault, the agonising death did not come.

Asmodeus closed his fingers into tight fists and just stared down at the mud-encrusted, pathetic little boy.

"You," he glowered, a frown of disbelief on his pale brow. He sneered in disgust, looked out across the battlefield, shook his head and disappeared in a loud cracking noise.

Bobby lay panting across the scorched body of Claw, unsure as to what had happened.

"Bobby! Bobby!"

He was aware of Katy rushing to his side and helping him sit up. Then, together, they tended to the injured vampire. Easing him up, they manoeuvred him into a seated position. He placed his hands on their shoulders and nodded before doing as his nemesis had just done and gazed out across the battlefield.

What met his and the children's eyes was an amazing sight.

Not one construct remained standing.

There, in the middle of the marshland, Scorpion and Tigress stood barely upright but victorious. The two women grinned at each other and the redhead stepped towards the blonde to embrace her.

An unmistakable, horrific sound filled the ears of the onlookers and they cried out with Tigress as they watched the lance shoot out through Scorpion's chest. Tigress screamed louder and louder in words that Bobby and Katy did not understand as she desperately grabbed at her partner and dragged her limp form off the lance. Claw growled in a wrathful effort as he practically threw himself across the wetlands to where the remains of a near-dead construct were trying to pull themselves out of the marsh. He sailed through the air with his black cloak flapping behind him, giving him the appearance of a dark, ferocious flying beast and he landed solidly by the coagulating mess of clay, thrusting his face down into its midst, drinking heavily.

Bobby and Katy stumbled and staggered their way across the killing field to the inconsolable Tigress.

"Cassie! Cassie!" she wept, red streaks flowing down her cheeks. "No! No!" She buried her face into the neck of her dead companion and seemed to try to pull them close enough together in a vain attempt to forge them both into one.

"She's gone." It was Claw who spoke, quietly, accepting the dreadful thing that had happened. He lay a hand on the shoulder of the redhead who just gazed up at him with emptiness. She opened her mouth to speak, but nothing came. Tigress turned to look at the lifeless Scorpion once more, then back up to her king.

She did not move from her mourning.

Claw nodded in response to an unspoken request and rose to his feet. He limped over to the children. "Come with me."

Bobby and Katy followed him across the marsh, walking back to where they had left the horses, leaving the grieving woman with the body of her dead love.

"Is Tigress not coming?" Katy asked when they reached the stand of trees.

"No," Claw replied, collapsing on the dry grass, resting his forehead on the floor. "She is not."

"What will you do with Scorpion's body?" Bobby asked. "Does Tigress want to bury her?"

The male vampire was still for an uncomfortable moment, his face close to the green grass. Eventually, he rolled over onto his side, his eyes staring out across the marshland. Bobby saw the same red tracks coursing down his cheeks.

"That will not be necessary. We vampires are curious creatures," he whispered. "Daylight will eventually come."

Bobby frowned, recalling what Claw had said about their few weaknesses. "Then Tigress needs to come with us and we must get to safety."

Claw continued to stare out across the empty space. "When we are born to this life," he continued, "it is not an easy birth. We have a dream, a nightmare. We see the very moment of our final death. It haunts us through our long lives as we wonder to ourselves, *is this the day?*"

Katy knelt next to the vampire and dragged his cloak around him. "What was Tigress' dream?" she asked.

"I think you both know."

So the three of them remained in that place and watched the long night away. They sat there as the cruel rays of sunshine began to creep across the horizon in the east. The children covered the weak vampire as best as they could, leaving him a small gap in his cowl through which he could watch the terrible sight of a final lovers' embrace.

As the sun rose, bringing life to the plants upon which it shone, Tigress drew herself closer to her loved one. She did not make a sound as smoke began to drift up from her shoulders, from her short red hair. She did not cry out as her skin began to catch aflame and fire danced across her form. She did not scream as that flame erupted in a fierce fireball, consuming her and the woman in her arms, sending them both to their final fate.

Chapter Six

The children and the vampire had to remain where they were for the best part of the next day as Claw's wounds healed themselves. Barely a word was said, just occasionally a member of the party would stare out across the barren marshland and sigh deeply before feeling the comforting weight of another's hand on their shoulder.

Bobby found the healing properties of Claw quite extraordinary. After Tigress and Scorpion had died, he had insisted that he check the vampire over. Claw had protested but, when Bobby's insistence was bolstered with that of Katy's, he had relented and they had carefully inspected his wounds, wincing at the savage scorch marks on his flesh.

"It's nothing," Claw had reassured

them. "They are just superficial. I will be fine to travel in a few hours. Most likely by to-night."

By midday, Bobby noticed that Claw began to move more. Not only was the vampire testing the strength of his arms and his legs but his burns were noticeably fading. Bobby ventured over to the horses and rummaged in the saddlebags for food. He dug out some cooked meat from their meal at the three-cornered tower, walked over to Katy, who was sat looking out across the marsh, and offered her some.

She just looked down at it and shook her head.

Well, that wasn't good.

"Katy?"

His sister said nothing and just resumed her vigil.

Bobby eased himself down onto the grass and sat cross-legged next to the eight-year-old. "There was nothing we could have done. There were too many constructs."

"Then there should have been more vampires." Her voice was small but resolute. Bobby could not miss the cold edge to it.

"There are no more. They were the last three."

"They should have made me one when I asked. I could have fought. With four of us, we would have had a better chance of success. Tigress and Scorpion…" Her words drifted off.

"Would still have died. You heard what Claw said. They knew how they were going to die."

Katy shook her head violently from side to side. "No. No. I can't believe that. We would have been able to change it. If I had been a vampire, I could have fought. I would have split those monsters open and drained them dry.

"And I would have enjoyed it!"

They were aware of a sound behind them. Claw had risen to his feet and was tentatively limping over to join them. "Katy, your brother is correct. There is nothing that we could have done. It was their time to die. No matter how many Children of Cain had been in that battle, the outcome would have been the same. No, all we can do is carry on with our quest. We must find Sam Spallucci.

He is out there. I know it. I feel it."

Bobby frowned. "You mentioned him the other night, at the tower. Who is he?"

Claw's brown eyes looked off to somewhere that the children could not see. "An old friend. I knew him when I was first made a vampire. My transition was not exactly by the book and Sam helped me through, reuniting me with my mother. He has been a good friend to the Children of Cain.

"And we treated him awfully." He shook his head.

"What do you mean?"

The vampire grimaced, rolling a shoulder as he did, testing it for mobility as he considered his reply. "To use a phrase that Sam detested, *it's complicated.* Timelines were involved and it was believed crucial that he did not know certain matters from the future so as not to disrupt them. He was kept intentionally in the dark about crucial matters.

"This led to a certain amount of friction between him and the others."

"But not you two?"

Claw shook his head. "No. He was a

good man and a good friend. And more."

"What do you mean?" Katy asked, finally tearing herself away from her vigil and joining the conversation.

Claw opened his mouth to speak but hesitated as his nostrils flared and he swivelled around, albeit unsteadily, drawing his knife as he did so. Bobby's and Katy's eyes were drawn to movement in the undergrowth as a familiar figure emerged from the dark shadows.

"The vampire means that he believes Spallucci is the Man of Virtue," Cutter explained in his usual grizzled voice as he stamped his way out of the overgrown thicket and into the midst of the three companions. "What's more he would lead you on a fool's errand to try and find him."

"Cutter!" Katy squealed at the sight of the old-timer and she tried to run towards him, but Claw's free hand darted out and gripped her shoulder, dragging her back.

"It's okay," Bobby reassured the vampire. "He's our friend. We know this man."

Claw's lips drew back as he exposed his fangs. "Trust me, that *thing* you see there is neither your friend nor a man."

The children turned back to Cutter and their faces changed from ones of confusion to ones of shock as the old man's features began to ripple and moisten, transforming into something else. In a moment, the old man had disappeared. In his place stood something quite different. Clad in long, obsidian black robes, smooth-skinned and with slicked-back hair stood a Shadow Wraith.

But not just *any* member of the elite corps of constructs. The face of this particular one, its black eyes peering down at him, was one that Bobby knew well.

It was the one that had murdered his father.

Bobby Normal will return in
Bobby Normal and the Fallen.

Author's Notes

Welcome to the end of the third adventure for our intrepid orphans. Once again, I hope it has answered some questions for you whilst leaving you hungry for more revelations that are yet to come.

The political philosopher Hobbes wrote in his magnum opus *Leviathan* that the life of man in the state of nature was "nasty, brutish and short." If you change that to "nasty, brutish and sometimes incredibly long" I feel it sort of summarises the lives of the vampires in my ever-expanding Spallucciverse. I fall into the same camp as Bobby. I think the idea of knowing how you will die must be an awful burden. There must be that constant thought at the back of your head of "is this the day?" I explored this in *Sam Spal-*

lucci: Dark Justice with the titular Child of Cain as he worked with Sam, even though he knew that this meant that he was now close to death as he had seen Lancaster's investigator of the paranormal in his dream.

The Children of Cain we see here in Bobby's world are somewhat different to those that Sam encountered in our contemporary world. Their personalities are still the same: Tigress is boisterous; Scorpion is long-suffering; as for Claw… I hope the eagle-eyed constant readers will have worked out who he is. However, their whole raison d'être has been blown out of the water. As Tigress quite succinctly points out, they had three tasks and they failed on all three counts. They are left rudderless, wandering the Divergent Lands taking out random constructs whilst Claw is insistent that Sam Spallucci is still alive and is indeed the prophesied Virtuous Man.

I have author friends who take great delight in killing off their characters. I am not one of those writers. My characters, even the darker ones are all my babies and it pains me when the time comes for them to die. As with most things in my Spallucci-verse, I plan ahead and I knew exactly how Tigress and Scorpion were going to go out from the moment that they first graced the pages of the short story *Girls Just Wanna Have Fun*. They were hunters, killers and would die doing what they did best; taking on overwhelming odds and revelling in it. Having said that, it was heartbreaking for me as I had to kill not just one beloved character, but two. I wrote the whole battle scene in one sitting and made myself battle on to the end because I knew that, if I was to stop, I would start to make excuses and avoid the final terrible act. If it brought a tear to your eye, then I think I did them justice.

So, we are now over halfway with Bobby, with just two of his adventures in the Divergent Lands left to play out. Whilst writing *BNCC*, I am also working on *Sam Spallucci: Fury of the Fallen*, which sees Sam pitting his wits against Asmodeus and Asherah in contemporary Lancaster. It's no accident that the next Bobby Normal book will see him stand toe to toe against the same characters.

I would be curious to know where you think Bobby's adventures will take him. Is there really a Virtuous Man? Is Sam Spallucci still alive? Will Katy get her wish and become a vampire or perhaps someone even more powerful might woo her over? Then of course there was the climactic reveal that Cutter is in fact the Shadow Wraith that executed Bobby's father, Howard.

Answers to some of these might be revealed next time…

ASC March 2022.

About The Author

A.S.Chambers resides in Lancaster, England. He lives a fairly simple life of walking in the countryside, gazing at mountains and rescuing his cat from the net curtains.

He is quite happy for, and in fact would encourage, you to follow him on Facebook, Instagram and Twitter.

There is also a nice, shiny website:
www.aschambers.co.uk